KĒROTAKIS

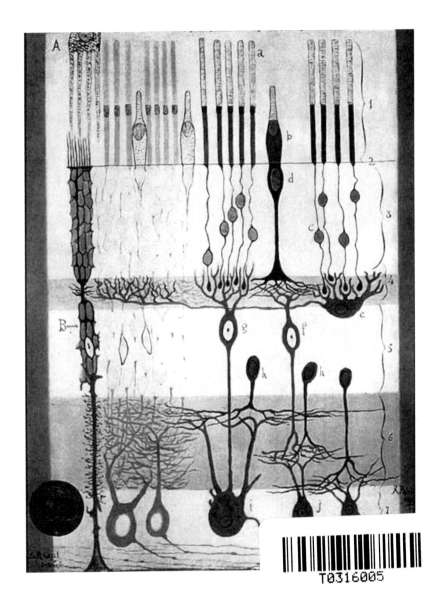

by janice lee

First edition published by Dog Horn Publishing, 2010

DOG HORN PUBLISHING
45 MONK INGS
BIRSTALL
BATLEY
WF17 9HU
United Kingdom

doghorn.com / editor@doghornpublishing.com

Todo hombre puede ser, si se lo propone, escultor de su propio cerebro.

(Each man can be, if he so determines, the sculptor of his own brain.)

-Santiago Ramón y Cajal

CAST OF CHARACTERS.

G.I.L.L.^{0}: a cyborg in the future

Dr. Eynan: a scientist in the past

Brain: the real brain of Dr. Eynan who is traveling
through time

Zosimosa^1: a Painter, an Author, a Mother out of
time

[0]G.I.L.L. is a cyborg. But she could be a human. *Could* is a helping verb. *Be* is a linking verb. It links *she* to *human*. *A* implies a definite singularity. It modifies human, G.I.L.L. as a human is a singularity. In time and in space.

[1]Zosimosa views alchemy as providing the means by which nature itself can pass from an imperfect state to a regenerate one. Zosimosa makes a kērotakis, a painter's palette, and henceforth she is also a painter.

The Latin term for torture is *crucifixion*.
Cruciatus includes anything from flogging to
strangulation. The crucifixion of mercury
then is any severe treatment that causes it
to change form. In the *Tractatus paraboli-
cus*, there is a detailed comparison between
the transformation of mercury and the tor-
ments of Jesus. As Jesus was first beat until he bled, then made to wear the crown of
thorns, then nailed to a cross, and treated
with gall and vinegar- so too must mercury be tortured in four distinct stages.
When mercury reddens during the process of
cooking, that redness denotes the body of
Christ.

The Four Aspects of
G.I.L.L.'s Crucifixion:

creation

                cleaning

        forced sight

                        escape

String theory suggests that the Big
Bang was not the origin of the
universe but simply the outcome of a
preexisting state.

this is some color but what color is this color, what is a color and which is this?

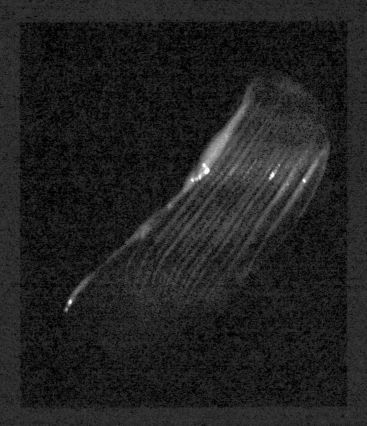

the
painter's palette
allows one

to paint, color, create. listen, listen.
there is somebody new to listen. sulfur
is sublimed. radical changes are made, so
listen to your mother. (she) draws the
nub, the connecting point that should not,
will not, exist in anything but colors and
words. take an easy sweep at her. don't
mistake it, this is not a sign of affec-
tion. she will leave the house first thing
in the morning. (she) will weep and watch
and continue listening.

(She) is Zosimosa,

who paints corpus hermeticum in red.
The body is the prison for the soul.
(She) does not differentiate between
man and dirt, flesh and rock, blood
and metal. And therefore she does
not differentiate between the sin of
man and the impurities of matter. As
(wo)men must or must not undergo a
spiritual chastisement for her sins,
metals are alchemically purified. Tell
me, brain in my brain, brain in my
heart. Sometimes I can not tell one
from another, or one from mine.

What would it be like to b l e e d , to
tend, to wake? What would it take to
make a place, to live in a place, to
live in a home, dreaming, calling, and
nothing coming?

Blood is not so rare, not so hard to come
by. The hours of killing and beating,
the splatter of red and coagulating
desire, it is not so hard to mimic.

In Leonardo da Vinci's manuscript B,
there is a recipe for *bel crocum ferri*.
This beautiful red pigment is made by
dissolving iron filings in impure nitric
acid, distilling off the solution and
calcining the residue. This is a more
complicated method of reddening waters,
reddening *the* waters, bloodying waters.
And too, similar methods can be used to
tinge works of gold.

Warning: Not all that glitters is
gold.

Zosimosa draws the bedsheets back. Yes, (she) will visit. And (she) will watch her bloom into a thousand flowers.

(She) writes, *She craved a mother's touch and milk. She touched her walls motherly and recalled an image of a cow. She tried to rewind and rewind but the tape would go no further. Was the lake shrinking? Was something missing or damaged? She could not remember.*

(She) paints red on the walls and lets out a small howl.

Does anybody listen?

She has a dot on her forehead.

The dot stands for zero, and so she
imagines it must increase her
beauty tenfold.

I need to be prepared to leave
tomorrow, to see truth, to cooperate,
to listen, to relate, to misplace...

G.I.L.L.:

Sometimes when they clean me, they are unkind. They forget to switch certain things off or on. I start to see many things at once. They project things for tests, to see the picture quality, frame rate, color saturation. Once I looked over at the screen with my eye, even though I already knew what was on it. The pain was unbearable. A luminous star exploding in my head. My eye is a camera, and you do not point a camera at a TV screen.

I am a walking surveillance camera.

G.I.L.L.:

Dear Self: I can have no nightmares of paternal abuse. I had no parents to guide me through an adolescence. There was no lump of matter to shape like clay. I sprouted instantly; my eye - it recorded that instant and more. The tape starts there. From blackness, color; from nothing, something. Was this how the world was created?

G.I.L.L.:

They tell many stories of whistles and names, words trailing me from room to room. But there is only one room, cramped with rulers, neat without dust. I go to the door and hear the dogs calling but they call for each other. I roam, my feet dragging in the sand, ending up next to a cactus in the desert. What makes a desert? The fact that there is sand? Or the fact that it is deserted?

The story that scares me most is the one about the Golem. The Golem is an artificial being who is brought to life by magic. After certain prayers, a small figure of a man is made from clay. They say the *shem hamephorash*, or name of power, over the figure and the figure comes to life. The figure cannot speak but it listens very well and understands what is commanded to it. It is made to serve its makers, taking care of all the household chores, and is not allowed to leave the house. On its forehead, they write *emeth*, which means truth. But the little man-like figure grows each day, outgrowing in volume all of its makers. To take away its strength, they quickly erase the letter *alef* from the word *emeth* on its forehead, so that there remains only the word *meth*, which means, dead. With this deed the golem collapses and dissolves back into clay.

Alef is a silent letter, whose sound
is as undetectable as the invisible
air.

G.I.L.L.:

I do not wish to return to dust and words, will this happen to me too? The Golem only has power in function but is so readily destroyed. The maker need only language to create, and like Frankenstein, there was never a request to be given entry into this world. *Return to your dust, return to your dust.* I only want a hand and perhaps a warm welcome. I will receive neither. The trees are only crooked but my sight is not. I am not an ogre but I live in a cave and sit like one. Only inches away an ant crawls across the floor.

I notice everything, and so do they.

G.I.L.L.:

There is something which it is like to be a human
being.

There is something which it is like to be a bat.

There is something which it is like to be me.

Life is a gesture, a series of gestures, a gesture of gestures,
waves of the wave, seeds into words, within and swept
up, a survival of demands. Do I know myself? Always,
it seems, in the form of something other, something
strange. I can't be honest because I don't fully know
what I am, peering out from a center which I cannot see,
gesturing another gesture.

G.I.L.L.:

I wonder of a home, a family habit, a turning away. The dot is as black as shadows and I wish I could look into a mirror to see the blackness multiplied forever.

I have made my nest in the desert. There is so much sand and dirt. Is the dust here the same as the dust[0] there? Is it my own skin that clings to the lens, or has the dust, the dry skin of millions of others followed me here? *I can not stay long.* I have a dialogue[1] with a cactus. They will find me. What I see is recorded, they will watch it from their tiny rooms- the walls closing in on them but never completely collapsing. If one leaves, another will take his spot. He is watching now, the prickly cactus in full focus, center frame, medium shot. He sees the camera pan over to a new frame of nothing but sky and sand. A transport approaches. Does he see it first or do I?

[0]Return to your dust, for this is a story of failure.
[1]*Have you seen my mommy?*

Dr. Eynan:

The trick is to catch a black hole in orbit around another luminous star. The orbit of the visible star will betray the presence of an unseen companion and the star will have material steadily pulled from its outer region by the companion's gravitational pull.

the box that can never be empty:

Dr. Eynan[0] tries to empty a box, but the box can never be empty. He sets up an empty box whose walls possess a finite temperature. The walls of the box radiate particles to fill the vacuum[1].

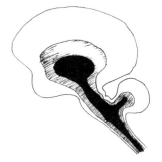

0Eynan is considered by Julian Jaynes to be the first god. The skeleton of this dead king of 9000 BC was found propped up on a pillow of stones by excavations in 1959. Jaynes suggests that the dead king was in the hallucinations of his people still giving forth his commands, a dead king becoming a living god.

[1] A vacuum is a volume of space that is essentially empty of matter, such that its gaseous pressure is much less than standard atmospheric pressure.

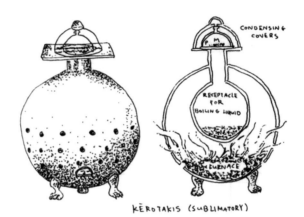

KĒROTAKIS (SUBLIMATORY)

Dr. Eynan tries to build his own
kērotakis,
or painter's palette.
He seeks results.   He seeks meaning[0].
He seeks consequence.   If his vessel
could sublimate some substance, he could
radically change the properties of one
substance using the vapors of another[1].
He could initiate change.   He could
produce radical changes in the colors
and properties of different substances,
metals, even flesh.

[0]Dr. Eynan thinks to himself, *Why can't I differentiate between something that has meaning and something that has no meaning?*
[1]*Papa, papa. Does it look good? Papa, papa. Can you hear me?*

(She) reads in the *Book of Hermes*:
the works of man can be both natural
with regard to essence and artificial
with regard to mode of production.

(She) wonders which is simpler:
having a distant mother or having a
dead one. (She) covers G.I.L.L. in
a red pigment using only a touch and
a w h i s p e r .

G.I.L.L.:

I am living by

l e t t e r s

on pages and words from mouths.

Silence can **stutter**
too,
and if so, if I stutter, if I stutter in the stuttering silence,
what can be heard that is clear?   Mother dear, I am
listening, but I can not hear anything.

There is always excess. I have to be cleaned weekly. They
go inside and suck up all the dust that has collected in
my workings, they wipe my lens clean- starting from the
middle and working outwards, pushing away the dust
that has collected there too.

I've heard that dust is 70% human skin. Whose skin?
Does that include my skin? Or is it all theirs?

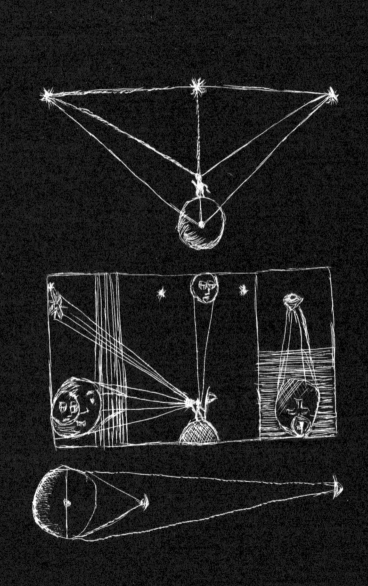

G.I.L.L.:

Flying through a mineral landscape and the tide[0] is coming in. *I'm ready to go*, I say. I do not mean it.

(She) tries to protect me. *Switch that off, switch that off!* (she) screams, when they subject[1] me to watching my own past footage. I ran away once and saw a cat with its innards pulled out in an alleyway. An uncanny tangle of blood and oil, intestines and shorted wires. They replayed it for three days. I tried to go through those days like any other ones, but the cat was everywhere. On the table, in the sky, in the trees, even in the sun. The overlap made it seem as if the sun itself was rotting away.

⁰Tide: deformation of a body by the differential gravitational force exerted on it by another body; in the earth, the deformation of the ocean (and to a lesser extent, of the land and air) by the gravitational pull of the Moon and Sun.

¹*Only of a human being and what resembles (behaves like) a living human being can one say: it has sensations; it sees, is blind; hears, is deaf; is conscious or unconscious.* (Wittgenstein)

Dr. Eynan will build a machine that will be able to send his brain through time. He first builds himself a replacement brain to keep him company while his real one is gone. He builds the machine, a tangle of wires and fluids and red pigments. The machine, using the anatomy, fluids, sparks, thoughts of the brain itself, will send the brain where Dr. Eynan can not go. Dr. Eynan instructs[0] the brain to send back signals, hints of its progress, numbers, observations, insights. Dr. Eynan makes the switch, and feels a little tickle[1]. The brain waves goodbye and then he is gone.

[1]Once the switch is made, Dr. Eynan is immediately not the good, old doctor anymore. Dr. Eynan 2.0 does not remember ever having made such a machine and does not remember such a switch and does not remember ever having instructed his old brain anything. Still, the doctor will go on to invent other new things. For example, he will reinvent the artificial brain and be applauded all around the world.

There is one, he has no second.

Dr. Eynan's Brain:

a metaphor for a
metaphor.

when I saw it was
a time I thought
where did that
time go
and then I
thought
where did I go

widowed brain in
only that which is
happening

           it is circling,   circling.
                            or,   orbiting.

will you monitor
an echo?

when is always
where is now

Dr. Eynan's Brain:

Hello.
Hello.

        Hello.
        Hello.

Hello?

Hello?

there is only the echo, echo.

(She) thinks G.I.L.L. must be the
visible   star,   and   that   unseen
companion must be the brain that
circles around in time in concentric
circles,
        circling
                ever
                        closer
                to a
                        destination.

G.I.L.L.:

How many mothers were born yesterday? How many
were mine?

G.I.L.L.:

Thou shall notice everything. This is my function, quoted from the Holy Texts, passed down by Deity Eynan. There is lava, lightning. I bunch up my face and ask to be thrown into a bucket, but they come anyway, never looking sweet or engaged.

Am I forgiven? I ask. They do not reply, only tell me that they are leaving now. I have seen the human students in their schools, chanting and repeating from the Texts all day long. Numbers are not important anymore. Only a select few need suffer such an education. The others only need to be able to tell when the woods are burning and where their homes are. It is not their job to notice when changes are made, and things are changing all the time.

Things have always been like this,
                    or at least a version of it.

G.I.L.L.:

What makes the wind blow so hard? Once the wind pushed me back so hard I could not propel myself forward. Breathing fast I flailed my arms like I was swimming, only to be gradually pinned down. I woke up later to their voices telling me that everything had been fixed.

When a glitch of any kind is detected, they can recreate me and my memory with everything they are constantly backing up. Am I so valuable? Or so dispensable?
I can not know if there has been change unless they tell me that there has been.

Memory is knowledge retained, not
knowledge stored.

She is undergoing constant changes,
seamless transitions.

She is constantly being reincarnated
from her own memories, and yet does
she experience a void during the
transition?

There is revealing in the desert, there is beauty in wide open spaces, there is exposure in wide spaces, there is space in wideness, there is sand in a wide space, there is beauty in sandy space, there is movement in beauty, there is movement in sand, there is nothing in movement, only movement, nothing to see, only movement. Set forth, there is little more to see in glass-making, revealing the light of the sun.

Excerpt from the Holy Texts:

T rue it is, without falsehood,
certain and most true.

That which is above is like to that which is below,
and that which is below
is like to that which is above,
to accomplish the miracles of one thing,
many things, or one thing[0].

And as all things were by contemplation of one,
so all things arose from this one thing
by a single act of adaptation[1].

The father thereof is the Sun[0],
the mother the Moon[1].

The wind carried it in its womb,
the earth is the nurse thereof.

It is the father of all works of wonder
throughout the whole world.

The power thereof is perfect[0].

If it/I be cast onto earth[1],
it will separate the element of water from that of fire,
the subtle from the gross.

[0]One grain, two grains, many grains.
[1]An emanating ratio, an act, and asking *Adapt to what?*

[0]This is a copy of something.
[1]The vapor is naturally moist and cold, exhalation warm and dry (I
breathe and breathe and breathe, musky breaths and sighs, over and
over again); and vapor is potentially like __, exhalation potentially like
__.

(She) reads:

1. *Copper is Whitened with Mercury-
Amalgam or Arsenic, and is then Colored
Golden by Electrum or Powdered Gold.*
Taking mercury, thrust it into the body
of magnesia or any white body, or of
unfired sulphur, or of silver spume, or
of quick lime, or to arsenic, and throw
in white (like the sky) earth of *Venus*,
and thou shalt have clear *Venus*; then
throw in yellow (like the sun) *Luna*, and
thou shalt have gold, and it will be gold
solder reduced into a body. Yellow (like
the sun) arsenic also makes the same, and
prepared red (like blood) arsenic, and
well bruised cinnabar, but quicksilver
alone makes brass shining; for nature
conquers nature.

2. *An Alloy of Gold is Heated by Superficial
Cementation.*
Treat Macedonian chrysocolla, which is
like the rust of bronze, and a babe from
the womb, by dissolving it in the urine of
a young girl until it entirely changes;
for the nature is hidden within. When,
therefore, it is changed, dip it into
castor oil, often heating it, and tinging
it, afterwards roast with alum, first
dissolving with unfired sulphur; render it
yellow (like the sun), and color the whole
body of gold; for nature rejoices with
nature, or, nature restrains nature.

G.I.L.L.:

Drawing circles in the sand, the sun cleansing every dark and earthy stain. Where is the blackness, the loosened earth, more than free, circling birds that come to say hello and then disappear again.

They see what I see and so I see carefully. In the desert it is often cold. Cold has power over the thick matter, because it has lost its heat, and the water is gone out of it. Then the dryness appears upon it, like sand on feet moving forward.

I do not have enough room to roam in here.

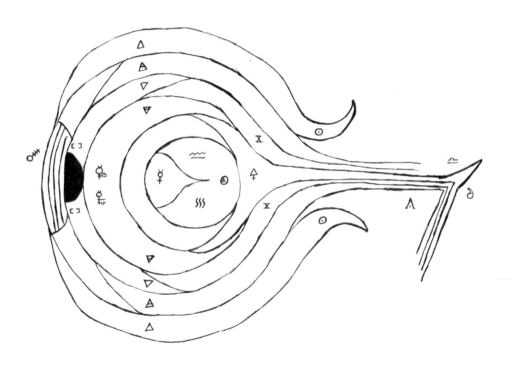

G.I.L.L.:

The parts withdraw themselves, whirring and dividing and buffing, striving to dry things up again with the heat.

I cannot remember being born. I cannot remember being brought home in a warm, green blanket. I cannot remember any warm welcome, any regret.

I remember seeing a picture:

> [Upon a dark violet field, a man red
> purple holding the foot of a lion red
> as vermillion, which has wings, and it
> seems would ravish and carry away
> the man.]

Decoded messages from Dr. Eynan's brain:

(note: these messages never make it back to Dr. Eynan, and instead, stay floating in the ether of time)

-from measuring temperature levels of different areas of human body is assumed that brain is major source of heat for body and heart is seat of emotion and intelligent thought.

- Mr. G theorizes that brain is organ of the mind and that mind is composed of multiple, distinct, innate faculties and that being distinct, each faculty must have separate seat / organ in the mind.

Decoded messages from Dr. Eynan's brain:

-*Text Book of Physiology,* on the relationship between spinal reflexes and the brain:

We may thus infer that when the brainless frog is stirred by some stimulus to a reflex act, the spinal soul is lit up by a momentary flash of consciousness coming out of the darkness and dying away into the darkness again; and we may perhaps further infer that such a passing consciousness is the better developed the larger the portion of the cord involved in the reflex act and the more complex the movement.

you're: conjunctions within the camera that perform/ occur on this level that I would lie on. the best combinations are the wrong combinations. the right combinations do not fit into the package. but either way, each combination will be analyzed and cut into other combinations. no matter the size, "you're" is always "you are" and "ARE" is the keyword because it IS.

performed: the actions of calling for the context of the situation. the context is always implied from something, or, the context is what you want it to be and therefore ... although there are those create-your-own-adventures, but those are even more contrived than these arbitrary combinations that utilize great performances.

lines: on the pavement. following on the way to the desert, just to find somewhere dry, dryer than this. it would be less of a problem if lines were straight.

achieve: nothing. it is inherent in these experiences that we enact over and over again. if act is to enact, and there are experiences, and there is art, and this twin of life, art. what do we transfer over when we are transferring colors from our mind to colors on this page, what are we achieving by this transfer?

everything: no matter if there was a disturbance in the space/time continuum no one would feel it. it is all relative they say and yet not really. those things with an origin are always more fragile when released and the stage that causes concern is the one right before the end of everything.

echo,   echo.

G.I.L.L.:

I went out into the trees one day and saw the flicker of a
knife. They were hollering as they pointed at me, and I
could do nothing to console these men that *they* would
not come for them now. I had seen them, and so had
they. These poor men would not make it through the
day.

I forgive you, one of their faces seemed to say. But I did
not need to be forgiven. *Faster, faster!* I tried to tell
them. As I looked over my shoulder, I noticed that the
lake was shrinking, and when I panned back over, they
were already gone.

Animals too can produce monsters when
their offspring do not belong to the
same race as the parents.

The basilisk is made from menstrual
blood sealed up in a flask and subjected
to the heat of a horse's womb. The
basilisk is a monster above all
monsters.

The basilisk, the wolf, and the
menstruating woman all have the
ability to fascinate, or, work harmful
magical effects by means of visual
emissions.

Jesus Christ was perhaps the first
homonculous, created in a sealed
vessel, or, Mary's womb.

G.I.L.L.:

There is red paint on my walls, on my lens, on my legs.
Am I menstruating? Or am I seeing red because I am
dirty? I did not know that I could bleed too.

How sure am I that this is how my
heart really goes *really I can try
and come home mama*, what eats sharks?
Get some sun, sit down, I'm not an
ogre but neither are you. We're just
like anyone and yet *a warm welcome*,
do you want to feel the cold? She's
asking and asking, *Is my mother dead
now?* I'm not finished yet. You think
I'm finished? Don't worry baby, Mama's
gonna hold you soon, *but when*, I'll
tell her, *listen, I'm bleeding red*,
the night is behind me too.

G.I.L.L.:

They make it easy for me, they give me my instructions.
I hold ground, always lock the gate behind, and watch.
I rarely speak to those lettered jars, scattered bodies of
full flesh. I want to be there when the desert blooms.
Something out of nothing. They envy us because we do
not sleep or eat or shit. Most of all, shit. The boundary
of my body is much more clear, the separation between
the internal, the external.

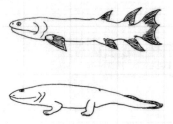

I undergo maintenance and they often probe around my
insides, listening and examining. My heart and brain
are part flesh, altered, maximized and reborn, thick and
frilled. When they go home, they draw the curtains and
have their privacy. That is one thing I will never have.

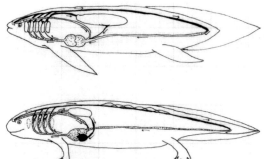

A dying star knows how to breathe underwater.

Decoded message from Dr. Eynan's brain:

Persistent habituation, (representing perhaps the
simplest form of m e m o r y) has been analyzed
in the defensive withdrawal reflex of the marine snail
Aplysia californica. The Aplysia
gill withdrawal reflex
is an involuntary, defensive reflex that causes the
organism's gill to be retracted when the animal is
disturbed by specific external stimuli.

the principle of the *virtus loci* –
the power of a particular place.

Dr. Eynan:

Matter: the solidity of matter is being dissolved into mathematical relationships in space. Could this be the same unphysical quality as the relationship of individuals conscious of each other?

Natural images tend to change relatively slowly over time.

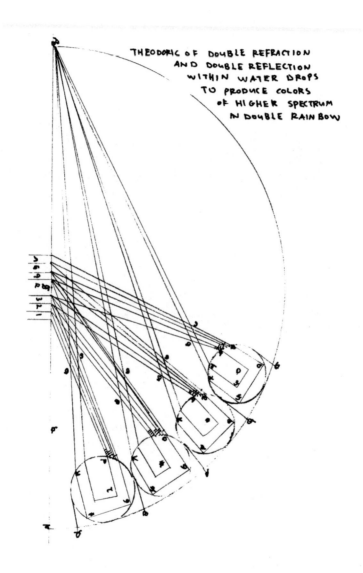

THEODORIC OF DOUBLE REFRACTION
AND DOUBLE REFLECTION
WITHIN WATER DROPS
TO PRODUCE COLORS
OF HIGHER SPECTRUM
IN DOUBLE RAINBOW

Dr. Eynan:

the empty space at the top of the mercury column.

the waking brain.

language growth by metaphor.

dinosaurs.

the glitch.

G.I.L.L.:

If the essence of technology[0] is by no means anything technological, where is my essence? When lightning strikes, will I fall or the tree[1]?

Am I a means or an end?

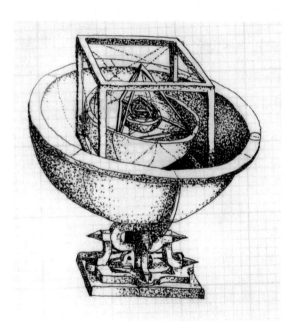

Do I cause or do I fall? Am I a cause or an effect? Am I just a sacrificial vessel, a knot in the rope, a middleman's tool, a donkey traveling through the desert?

[0] *Technology is a way of revealing.* (Heidegger)
[1] Up in the tree, there is a babe in the mother's arms. The babe cries out and the mother makes things all right again.

G.I.L.L.:

I am a way of revealing[0]. I reveal myself. I reveal color.
I reveal a reality. I unveil. I am unveil. I reveal. I am
revealed. I am revealing. I reveal an encounter[1].

⁰*All revealing comes out of the open, goes into the open, and brings into the open.* (Heidegger)
¹*In truth, however, precisely nowhere does man today any longer encounter himself, ie. his essence.* (Heidegger)

Excerpt from the Holy Texts:

With great sagacity
it/I doth ascend[0] gently
from earth to heaven.

Again it doth descend[1] to earth,
and uniteth in itself the force
from things superior and things inferior.

Thus thou wilt possess the glory
of the brightness[0] of the whole world,
and all obscurity will fly far from thee.

This thing is the strong fortitude of all strength,
for it overcometh every subtle thing
and doth penetrate every solid[1] substance.

Thus was this world created.

Hence will there be marvellous adaptations achieved,
of which the manner is this[0].

For this reason I am called Eynan,
because I hold three parts of the wisdom[1]
of the whole world.

⁰The precious metals originate from the imprisonment of the vaporous exhalation in the earth, especially in stones, especially in cramped cells.
¹*Daddy, have you come for me?*

[0] *Can the brightness of the desert be extracted?*
[1] Let the boundaries hold. Let that stay in and this stay out.

⁰This color is red but maybe it should be yellow.
¹*And He created His universe with three books, with text, with number, and with communication.*

Since everything that grows comes from
a seed, the fruit must be contained
in its seed.

Dr. Eynan:
(scribbled in notebook)

Manufacture of a Pearl.

Take and grind an easily pulverized stone such as window mica. Take gum tragacanth and let it soften for ten days in cow's milk. When it has become soft, dissolve it until it becomes as thick as glue. Melt Tyrian wax; add to this, in addition, the white of an egg. The mercury should amount to 2 parts and the stone 3 parts, but all remaining substances 1 part apiece. Mix and knead the mixture with mercury. Soften the paste in the gum solution and the contents of the hen's egg. Mix all of the liquids in this way with the paste.

Then make the pearl that you intend to, **according to a pattern.** The paste very shortly turns to stone. Make deep round impressions and bore through while it is moist. Let the pearl thus solidify and polish it highly.

If managed properly it will excel the natural.

G.I.L.L.:

He forms the year and sheds light on all beneath the sky, as I continue trudging, watching, scanning smoothly and gently. Only in the desert the beams seem to fill my insides with increasing warmth, a rapid course, summoning grains and heating the trees to bud. From the sun or to the sun or to the moon, shining orbs are fixed by a yellow principle, all bodies tinged by the color of the sun, and perhaps then something is revealed or hidden forever.

You can perceive large areas of space
and still remain aloof from them.
You do not actually have to be in a
portion of space in order to perceive
it. This is not true of time. You can
only perceive the time in which you
exist. You may perceive the past in
memory, or the future in imagination,
but direct perception only exists in
the present. You can perceive space
at a distance, but time only when in
proximity to it.

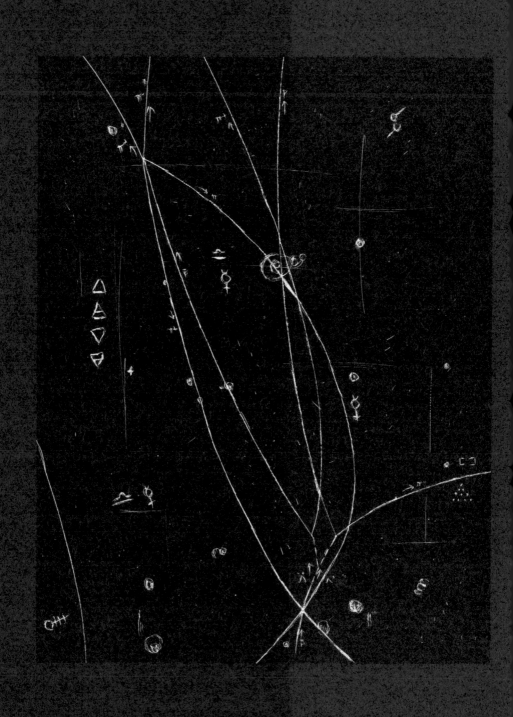

G.I.L.L.:

I may live in a macrocosm^0 or a microcosm^1, I may be a macrocosm or a microcosm, I may destroy such things, see such things, or *hush, be still little one.* These things, they all mirror each other, and when I look into the mirror, all I can see is the empty circle, a dot, a zero, a mark, or a great big world in which to live.

The last time I was in the desert, I curled up into a little ball and tried to close my eyes. As the blackness started to pervade, I felt myself being lifted up into the sky. I awoke on a hard, flat surface.

⁰The "great world" of man.
¹The "little world" of man.

[0]The "great world" of man.
[1]The "little world" of man.

__: What then is Alchemy?

__: It is the raising of vibrations.

In the humming (she) watches over,
feeling a distance, even with a caress.
The humming, only a mother could
hear, but (she) is not a mother, and
the girl will always be motherless,
only watching and laboring to their
beat beat beat.

(She) wants her cyborg to find a
passage, fly right. This is all a
phase. She has no father, no mother
after all. Her legacy is dust and
consciousness.

Can she disconnect?

Is she willing to swim, blind and
blinder. Hang the sheet out, a flag
in the yard, the birds are circling.
She could be one too.

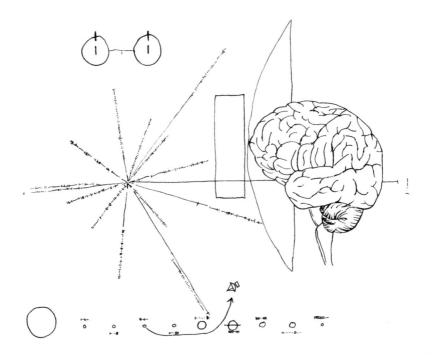

Dr. Eynan:

Did I need it first or could I tear it from my brain?

Decoded messages from Dr. Eynan's brain:

here is the distinction and here is the blurred edge of
distinct blurs.
                  but perception, how do I perceive the blurs?

moment to moment and there are transitions between the
cuts, the edits.
                  but in life, isn't every other moment a transition?
or, if it is one long take, are there no transitions at all?

and what can I really say, what do I really know if it is all
random and arbitrary and if what is invested is arbitrary,
or does it all reoccur like the concepts and are we part of
a reoccurring state of existence (so what does that do for
perception, what does that do for memory) and we will
never really know what came before or after.

lies are not secrets. they are lines drawn outside of lines
drawn outside of more lines.

orbiting, orbiting.

what?!

what truth?!

RECORDINGS FROM NEURON
IN PRIMARY VISUAL CORTEX

I live. live=active verb. how to make the passive? I was
lived. I have been lived. life lives me. I am lived. I am
alive. passive activity not active. not active-ity at all. where
to go from here?

Dr. Eynan's Brain:

consciousness and protozoa.   a writhing, a release, a
connection.

---

average firing rate:

$$\langle r \rangle = \frac{\langle n \rangle}{T} = \frac{1}{T}\int_0^T d\tau \langle p(\tau) \rangle = \frac{1}{T}\int_0^T dt\, r(t).$$

AVERAGE FIRING RATE:

$$\langle r \rangle = \frac{\langle n \rangle}{T} = \frac{1}{T}\int_0^T d\tau \langle p(\tau) \rangle = \frac{1}{T}\int_0^T dt\, r(t)$$

there is the shadow of the action.
there is autonomy.
which am I?

MEMORY PATTERNS $\rightarrow v^m$

$v^m \rightarrow m = 1, 2, \ldots N_{mem}$

NUMBER OF MEMORIES $\rightarrow N_{mem}$

MEMORY CAPACITY:

$$v^m = F(M \cdot v^m)$$

MEMORY NETWORK $\rightarrow K \cdot v^m = \lambda v^m$

FOR ALL m . . .

$$\rightarrow M = K - \frac{nn}{\alpha N_v} \quad \text{or} \quad M_{\partial\partial'} = K_{\partial\partial'} - \frac{1}{\alpha N_v}$$

RECURRENT WEIGHT MATRIX:

$$M = \frac{\lambda}{c^2 \alpha N_v (1-\alpha)} \sum_{n=1}^{N_{mem}} (v^n - \alpha cn)(v^n - \alpha cn) - \frac{nn}{\alpha N_v}$$

there is always a performance quietly occurring.

Decoded messages from Dr. Eynan's brain:

so these totem poles flickered in and out of thoughts and I couldn't tell what side of the glass I was on and then I wondered what it was that I was in denial of. was it that subject assigning me the denial that I was in denial about and if so, why couldn't I realize it. can I retain all this in terms of leaving, in terms of this long take called life, in terms of cuts and edits that I assign to myself and to others, wondering what a point of view really is and how arbitrary my point of view is, with or without eyes to see out of, and whether it all makes a difference if only for the edits and summation of these edits and memories that aren't memories but arbitrary moments ingrained mentally somehow and retaining some sentimentality that is also assigned somehow *(associations)*. perhaps only with guilt or this concept called emotion can I perhaps differentiate between something that has meaning and something that has no meaning.

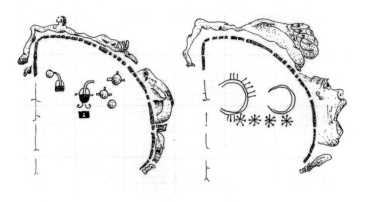

this **distinction** between the way I see the world,
and the way you see the world.

Decoded messages from Dr. Eynan's brain:

-Mr. Mithen states that before period of dramatic cultural change, humans possessed domain-specific mentality. ways of thinking and stores of knowledge about different cognitive domains were isolated from each other

--> cognitive domains.

-there existed the ability to explore these conceptual spaces / cognitive domains on individual basis but not to transform them by integrating modules of knowledge or ways of thought from different spaces / domains. the newly evolved ability that allowed this to happen was

--> cognitive fluidity.

-theory of mind.
behaviors that depend on possession of a theory of mind.

1. intentionally informing others
2. intentionally deceiving others
3. intentionally communicating with others
4. repairing failed communication with others
5. teaching others
6. intentionally persuading others
7. building shared plans and goals
8. intentionally sharing a focus or topic of attention
9. pretending

G.I.L.L.:

I am only spectator to the intermittent cries and whimpers, the changes in sudden jerky moments. At that stage exists something in the shape of a lake, moving with remarkable speed, unaffectedly lowering its flag in surrender. Is that what escape must be like?

Their protests are in vain, and I am unable to differentiate surfaces, or I am unable to lend a hand, a foot, a toe, a word. I am victim to the atmospheric drag in the narrow surface between threads and short, explosive coughs. The coughs are mine, and the coughs have no remedy except rest.

Dr. Eynan:
(scribbled in notebook)

Each kingdom has its own mercury, which manifests under different vibrations in each realm.

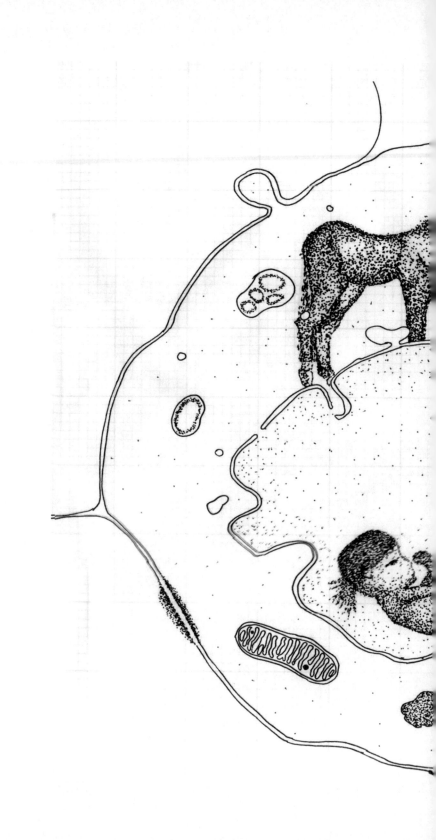

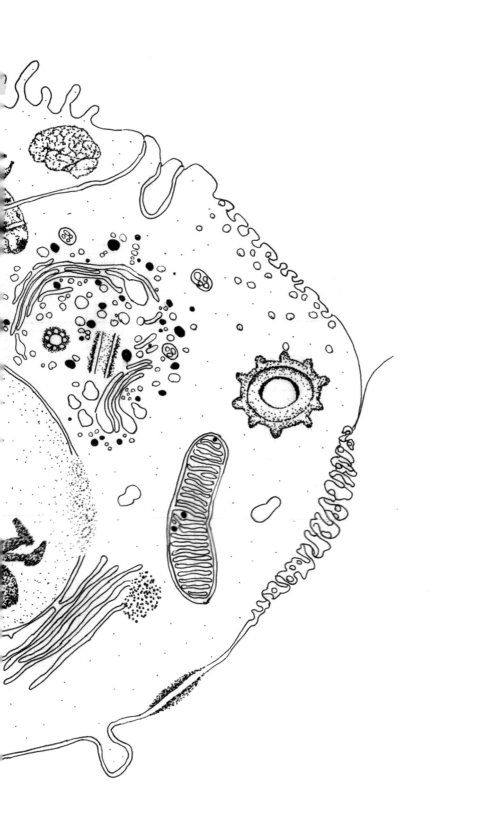

G.I.L.L.:

Am I vegetable[0], animal, or mineral[1]?

[0] Deep in the dirt, a watery vapor would nurture me, shape me, feel me, comfort me.
[1] Or like a stone, still, with essences imprisoned within.

G.I.L.L.:

There is a bird without wings who travels from home to home, bringing water as rain and breaths as wind. The bird has no wings but insists on flapping. He calls the sun its father and the moon its mother, and says that the wind carries him in its belly.

I saw that bird fall yesterday, still flapping, croaking, and speaking words. From its beak spilt a deep, red mercury, the same as found in all things.

Could I find a pair of wings somewhere, or perhaps build them out of rain and air?

G.I.L.L.:

How many revered symbols would continue to elude me in alternate realities, realities realer then some and not as real as others and as I entered the abode, could anything outside of these really be any better?

At what price can a moving island take precise aim at the mechanism that can render steel ineffective? When I assume the form of a flare, or find friendly sand, perhaps then my fears will be put to rest.

G.I.L.L.:

A bird, slanted across the sunlight, another one out of the bottle and a turn, a turn, a turn, another turn. A similar situation crossed me but I can't remember if I wanted to. There is beauty in wide open spaces.

G.I.L.L.:

Just symbols of restlessness, I do not relent. I am not free.
I imagine being taken for a moon ride by moonlight,
marked by the night, the black, and the night turning its
back on me only after the day told me I had too much
pride because I mix love and pity and anger and lust and
restlessness into the oceans as my heart pounds with the
wind and a broken pot shows my reflection cracked from
the morning sun.

Decoded messages from Dr. Eynan's brain:

I only know what I can touch
everything else
that
exists
is:

construction.

                    at the end of mind
                            is failure.

reality: that doesn't exist arbitrarily as a word and words are only words that swim in ethereal ether called language and within language there is some universality of black holes and time warps that spin back into backwards functions that reflect back onto backs and is *real* really *real*?

has: metal turns and I think about what I have given up or whether I have really given up anything at all and are all acts selfish and if so what is this pain I am drawn to and is the red on the wall the paint left over from trying to cover my heart.

its: belonging to something and some kind of dependency that highlights itself emphasizing self-identity that is merely chance and pages that flip and its density is not very thick nor will it congeal in time for supper.

own: bear descended from heavens and parted the clouds and said I want to live in this cave and eat and sleep and rest and the clouds floated around, circles in the air, breathing quietly and there is this realization that this is my own life and no one else's. or, is it simply a metonymy?

language: tourniquet around the tongue, the mind, disconnection from space space space a few more words ought to solve the problem of ambiguity, tangled hairs and thoughts and what are these words that come with ideas?

G.I.L.L.:

I wanted to get out from under the thumb.

Sometimes I feel all the way to my face, blustering words out to make those trees sing once more. Though they never did really and I think I can feel pain if I only smile a bit more.

It is always too soon for me, though I sit, watchful. What is it inside me that doubles and quickens?

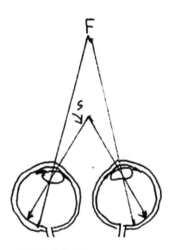

RETINAL DISPARITY.

G.I.L.L.:

A gate swings shut behind me, me going in, him going out. I imagine myself on his arm saying, *Daddy, will you guide me home?* I hold out my hand, but receive nothing in return. I hold my ground, always, noticing, noticing everything. A dog with a blinker of flesh over his right eye watches my movements. He is not the intruder here, I am.

I make my slow way down the mountain. Today, they tell me, I am probing for *stubborn donkeys who are a danger to the state.* These are the ones who did not go to school, or ran away. A pond, a rolling hill, a broken twig. And the whirring of a helicopter.

I would like: a warm welcome or a warm farewell.

G.I.L.L.:

I came across a lady once, her belly round and swollen. I thought to myself, *A baby grows in you.* And I thought, *What grows in me?* I imagined gouging the woman, pulling the stiff hair hatching from her head, and extracting the unborn fetus. I only imagined, I did not perform. But it recorded anyway.

What gets recorded is not necessarily the memory I retain. The recordings are complete, archived- though the organic part of my brain remembers with human flaws.

Identities have been known to fuse
and unfuse at particular points in
time and space.

Dr. Eynan's brain continues to circle, circle in time. It is circling ever closer to a destination, until, suddenly, it finds itself embedded in another consciousness. It injects into G.I.L.L. a strange, milky substance.

G.I.L.L.:

I am no longer the intruder. There is an intruder but it is not I.

Brain:

Where am I?

G.I.L.L.:

I am coming to be aware of your existence. Are you a gap or a being?

Brain:

I am neither a gap or a being. I am a brain.

G.I.L.L.:

Who's brain? Not mine[0]. Not theirs.

Brain:

A brain outside of time[1].

⁰*Are you my mommy?*
¹The brain knows perfectly well where and when he is, and has already pinpointed his particular place in space and time. He has already absorbed the data funneling from G.I.L.L.'s little brain and has already realized her direct relationship to his owner. Of course he has also realized that his owner has already forgotten about him, but, perhaps, this little encounter will help to ring a bell.

It is as impossible to produce a metal
out of a plant as to make a tree out
of a dog or a baby.

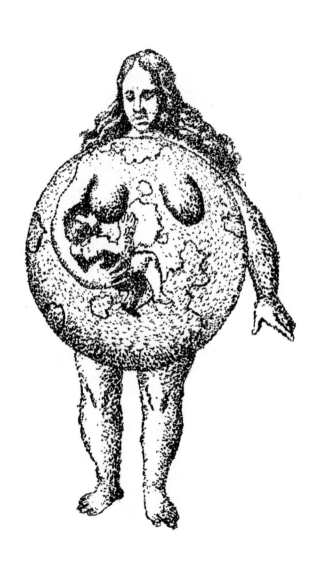

G.I.L.L.:

I saw my mother sleeping at the bend in the road, an asphalt pillow and yellow dotted lines. She was not my mother, maybe someone else's. The color red was soaking through the crotch of her hands. Her eyes looked inverted, pale and moaning. I had an urge to scrub her, especially the red. But in that moment, I was only a little bird, and my wing would not grasp a sponge. I hopped and stuttered away. The mother continued to moan behind me without a stutter.

The Golem must be made of virgin
soil, taken from a place where no
man has ever dug. The soil must
be kneaded with pure spring water,
taken directly from the ground. If
this water is placed in any kind of
vessel, it can no longer be used.

She sits in the desert, facing east, breathing and chanting letters. Between each letter she takes a single breath. Between pairs she takes two. She makes the head motions slowly and deliberately, as if she has been practicing them in her sleep, as if these motions have been passed down from mother to daughter.

She pronounces one letter and exhales, the motions corresponding to the shape of the vowel. She begins straight ahead, raises her head upward. She then begins from the right, moving her head to the left. Then from the left she moves her head to the right. She then begins by looking straight ahead again, and lowers her head downward. Finally, she moves her head directly forward, and waits.

Area MT[0] of the brain sees movement, follows suit, right, then left.

PPA[1] detects an unverified species of sand.

[0]Almost all the neurons in area MT (middle temporal area) are direction-selective, meaning that they respond selectively to a certain range of motion directions and do not respond to directions beyond that range.
[1]The PPA (parahippocampal place area) is category-selective and responds best to houses, landmarks, indoor and outdoor scenes.

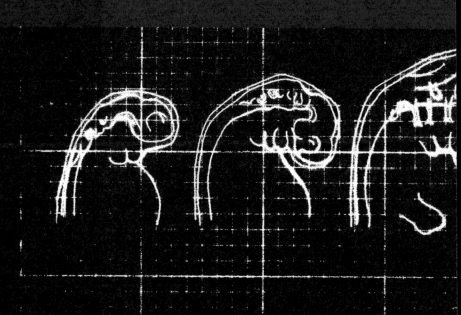

The brain is not an organ of
perception, even though, of
course, one cannot see, hear,
taste, smell or feel anything
unless one's brain is
functioning appropriately.

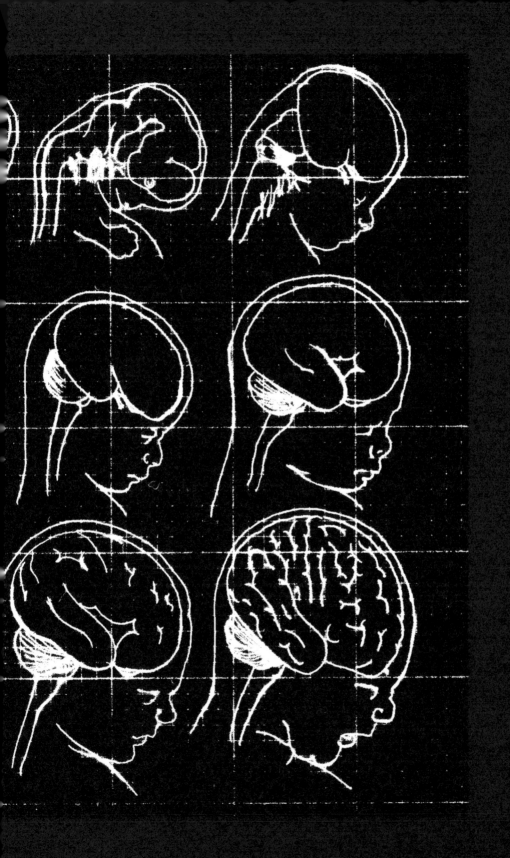

Brain:

One angel cannot have two missions. Neither can two angels share the same mission.

G.I.L.L.:

What if they cut out my tongue, what if I was just a hardened bump in a tube, what if I had fists instead of toes?

Brain:

The mind can only focus on one thought or memory at a time…

G.I.L.L.:

One bump, one box, one hair follicle.

Brain:

A thought and an angel, both rise like dim fog when the woods are burning. Angels have no way of knowing anything that does not pertain to their particular mission. An angel may be created initially with a vast storehouse of knowledge, but it has no way of increasing it, at least, not beyond its own sphere of activity. One angel may have to ask another angel a question, because he himself would not know something outside of his own domain.

G.I.L.L.:

A thought, a memory, an angel, a mule.

Brain:

In the physical world, people can learn things through their five senses. They can hear, feel, smell, and taste. Knowledge of things comes from a physical proximity to them. But in the spiritual world, this does not exist. The only way one can learn about a thing is to come into spiritual proximity with it. An angel cannot do this outside of his own realm.

G.I.L.L.:
(a little bit tired, runs her fingers through the sand)

Brain:

Man therefore has an advantage over an angel. The very fact that he exists in this lower world enables him to reach up ever higher. Man can move from level to level, but angels are bound to their particular plane.

G.I.L.L.:

But am I an angel?

G.I.L.L.:

The sun sets red[0], *is it bleeding?* The sky can not be measured, but there are ideas[1] spurting out of heads all of the time.

They merely accept the concepts presented to them blindly, without inquiring into their rationality.

I am not a rational being. What time **is** it?

[0]Red vibrates at a rate of between 47,000,000,000 and 52,000,000,000 per second (or a wavelength of approximately 7,000 angstrom units), producing specific chromatic conditions in the retina, which constitutes a man-made concept of the physical actuality being described.
[1]Our terrestrial thinking occurs in time.

G.I.L.L.:

Do I look like you inside?

Brain:

I shouldn't think so.

G.I.L.L.:

Are you a copy? Is there a backup copy of you somewhere?
You seem valuable, there should be a backup.

Brain:

Stutter, stutter.

G.I.L.L.:

I saw a dead man with gold between his teeth[0].
Mercury has been administered to him throughout his
lifetime, and it is the nature of mercury to ascend to the
mound, speaking, telling, breathing, forming an outlet
and evacuating within the spittle. The sick man, having
had an unfortunate accident, the metal remaining in his
mouth between his teeth, the carcass becoming a natural
matrix to ripen the mercury, the body having been shut
up for a long time in a cave in the woods, the mixture
congealed into gold by its own proper sulphur, being
purified by the natural heat of putrefaction, caused by the
corrosive phlegm of man's body. This never would have
happened if mineral mercury had not been administered
to him. Was it his mother[1], his father?

Then, the blackness of black, the head of a crow, the
bottom of the glass.

Since Cause cannot exist without Effect, Effect is also the cause of Cause. In this sense, Effect is the cause, and Cause is the effect. Since beginning and end are inseparable, their end is embedded in their beginning, their beginning in their end.

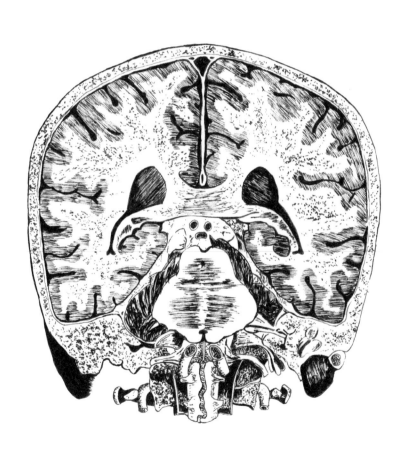

G.I.L.L.:

I miss the mineral stink of dirt, the outside. In here the walls are too smooth. The lights are not warm. They expose, radiate. Only a metallic sheen, the only real color is white. My hand rides each surface, glossed and slick, tarnished silver.

I c r e e p along edges, no twitches. I absorb essences. Where is my home?

G.I.L.L.:

It is cold out tonight. I can not feel it, but the pipes are frozen and I can see that. (Her) breath comes out like smoke, clean and smoothly. (She) does not sleep, but who can sleep? A spluttering, breathing being. I think to touch (her) but she is deep in thought, planning out her characters. I go outside and touch the building instead, scratched and settled. I peel back aluminum and notice boot prints on the ground. I am kept here at this harbor, free of rust. My own vision, my mind, my sight- those are my anchors. A hanging sheet flutters in the wind, birds circling around. Where is the lighthouse?

G.I.L.L.:
(a little bit tired, a little bit weary, places her hand on the ground)

Are we safe here?

Brain:

Perhaps you should sit down.

G.I.L.L.:

But, no, it's nothing. It's just, I'm tired.

Brain:

Yada yada yada yada.

G.I.L.L.:

Get away, get away!

Brain:

What are you doing? I think the wind is blowing in from the sea.

G.I.L.L.:

Looking for eggs in the sand. This seems like a good hiding place, someone must have gone to the trouble of hiding eggs in this sand. I want to find one, before I have to go back. Am I dreaming?

Brain:

Everything is shining, throwing off light from the sand. I may have somewhere to go soon.

G.I.L.L.:

Me too.

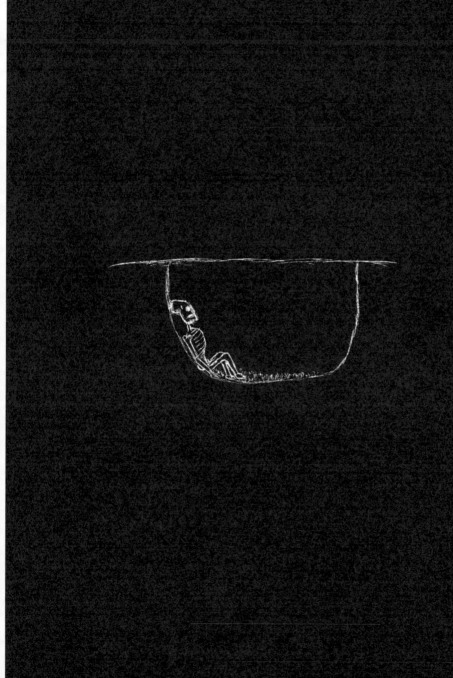

As soon as the influence of the mind ceases, the heart ceases to function, this being the definition of death.

G.I.L.L.:

Two children construct a snowman but I don't yet understand why a snow*man*. It has no legs and crumbles to the touch. What man has such dark eyes, such coldness in his belly, such inability to move. When they constructed me, they thought of efficiency, movement, perception. This snowman has nowhere to go. Its lifespan is short. But it is free to sit and observe happenings without fear of consequence.

Dr. Eynan:

Who is this?[0]

G.I.L.L.:

Who is this?[1]

．

[0]And with this, Dr. Eynan suddenly remembers what he did with his brain.

[1]And with this, G.I.L.L. for a slight moment experiences a new sort of consciousness, mediated by Dr. Eynan's brain, and momentarily communes with The Creator. And with that experience, and with the return of Dr. Eynan's memory, Dr. Eynan immediately brings his brain back to his time and place, leaving G.I.L.L. a used, empty vessel.

G.I.L.L.:

It was the little man with the burned feet who realized
the Golem was a Golem and told it to *return to the dust*,
because not just anyone can make a monster speak.

This is a two-way street.

There are two types of storm winds.
One that merely agitates. And
another, a hurricane, that sweeps
away everything in its path. This
second kind is the one that carries
the brain a w a y.

Chaos is a state where information can exist, but where it does not exist. G.I.L.L. is now a vacated space, a space where it is possible for information to exist, but where this possibility has not yet been realized. G.I.L.L. is stuck at some point between a death and a birth. She can remember neither of these, and so, does not know which direction she should go.

G.I.L.L.:

I do not remember my first birth, but this is my second.
What comes before one? Is one again.

Water from Breath:

There is a letter, any letter, or a
particular letter.

She then begins to see the letter as if
she were looking at it through water.
This is *drawing it through water*. The
letter then begins to blur and fade, as
if it were being viewed through
increasingly deeper waters. *Deeper and
deeper, take a plunge my darling, Mommy
is coming for you.* There is engraving,
chaos and void, mire and clay. The form
breaks up, dissolves completely, as if
seen through turbulent water, then fades
away completely, *the water is muddy now.*
This is mire.

All that is left is inky blackness, she
feels as if buried in thick mud and
clay. She is covered like a ceiling,
blackness beneath her feet, her feet
dissolving away, the blackness creeping,
creeping over her, and surrounding her
like a wall. She feels nothing,
remembers nothing. She is only
constantly aware of the feeling of water
and absolute calm.

It is the dark, wet feeling of the

womb, where she is totally isolated
from all sensation.

Water conceived and gave birth to
absolute darkness.

G.I.L.L.:

I lie in my bed quivering. What will become of me?
Do I continue to tremble? The trembling is movement.
Movement means live, moving forward. Which direction
to shake. I just want to be still.

G.I.L.L.:

My turn is over.

CREDITS.

Image References:

Ramon y Cajal, Santiago. "Structure of the Mammalian Retina" c.1900

Berthelot, M. *Introduction a L'étude de la Chimie*. 1889. Chrysopée de Cléopâtre, figure 11.

Cloquet, Jules. *Manuel d'anatomie descriptive du corps humain, représentée en planches lithographiées*, 1825. cited in Rifkin, Benjamin A. and Michael J. Ackerman. *Human Anatomy*. Henry B. Abrams,Inc. 2006.

Dayan, Peter and Abbot, L.F. *Theoretical Neuroscience: Computational and Mathematical Modeling of Neural Systems*. MIT Press, 2001.

Dwiggins, Don. "History's first 'Space Station" from 1784." *Into the Unknown: The Story of Space Shuttles and Space Stations* San Carlos: Golden Gate Junior Books, 1971.

Ginger, Ray (Ed.) *Spectrum: The World of Science*. Henry Holt and Company, 1959,
        p24 Eusthenopteron, Ichthyostega.
        p27 Gills in fish and amphibians.
        p50 Production and Decay of Strange Particles.
        p52-53 The living cell, diagram by M. Broyer, 1957; courtesy of W. Stoeckenius.

Gray, Henry. "Fig. 351–Transverse vertical section of the brain." *Gray's Anatomy*. New York: Bounty Books, 1977 (15th ed). p657.

Howell, F. Clark. *Early Man*. Time-Life Books: Life Nature Library, 1965, p139 Combe Grenal in detail, Diagram of Layer 21.

Kepler, Johannes. "Prodromus Dissertationum Mathematicarum Continens Mysterium Cosmographicum." *Mysterium Cosmographicum*. 1596.

Maier, M., *Atalanta fugiens, Oppenheim,* 1618

Newman, William R. *Promethean Ambitions*. University of Chicago Press, 2004,

p31 Modern reconstruction of a *kērotakis* as conceived by F. Sherwood Taylor, based on *Marcianus graecus* 299, fols. 112r and 195v.
p245 Theodoric of Freiberg's illustration, from a late medieval manuscript.

Reisch, Gregor. *Pretiosa Margarita*, Basle, 1508.

de Sacrobosco, Johannes. *Sphaera Mundi, Antwerp.* 1573.

Sagan, Carl and Drake, Frank (Design); Sagan, Linda Salzman.. "NASA image of Pioneer 10's Pioneer plaque," "Ames Pioneer 10." *NASA.* 1972.

Sensory homunculus, Motor homunculus. www.in-mind.org/images/stories/homunculus.png

Textual References:

Albertus, Frater. *Alchemist's Handbook.* Red Wheel/Weiter, 1974.

Baars, Bernard J. (Ed.) *Cognition, Brain, and Consciousness.* Academic Press, 2007.

Barrow, John D. *The Book of Nothing.* Vintage Book, 2000.

Bennet, M.R. and Hacker P.M.S. *Philosophical Foundations of Neuroscience.* Blackwell Publishing, 2003.

Foster, Michael. *A Textbook of Physiology.* London: Macmillan, 1890.

Heidegger, Martin. *The Question Concerning Technology and Other Essays.* Harper & Row, 1977.

Jaynes, Julian. *The Origin of Consciousness in the Breakdown of the Bicameral Mind.* Mariner Books, 1976.

Kaplan, Aryeh. *Sefer Yetzirah: The Book of Creation.* Red Wheel/Weiser, 1997.

Linden, Stanton J. *The Alchemy Reader.* New York: Cambridge University Press, 2003.

Mithen, Steven J. "Chapter 10: A Creative Explosion." *Creativity in Human Evolution and Prehistory*. Routledge, 1998.

Newman, William R. *Promethean Ambitions*. University of Chicago Press, 2004.

Plato. *Timaeus*. (ca. 360 BC).

Ruland, Martin. *A Lexicon of Alchemy*. London: J. M. Watkins, 1964.

Scholem, Gershom. *Alchemy and Kabbalah*. Spring Publications, 2006.

Veneziano, Gabriele. "The Myth of the Beginning of Time." *Scientific American* May 2004.

Wittgenstein, Ludwig. *Philosophical Investigations*. Prentice Hall, 1973, (§281).

ACKNOWLEDGEMENTS.

The author would like to thank the following people for their support:

Jon Wagner, Matias Viegener, Christine Wertheim, Anna Joy Springer, Teresa Carmody, Vanessa Place, Bhanu Kapil, Will Alexander, Jen Hofer, Laura Vena, Joseph Milazzo, Maxi Kim, Dante Zúñiga-West, Eugene Lee, Benny, and Jeff Uyeno.

And much gratitude to Adam Lowe and Dog Horn Publishing for making this happen.

ABOUT THE AUTHOR:

JANICE LEE's work can be found in *Zafusy, antennae, sidebrow, Action, Yes, Joyland, Tarpaulin Sky*, and *Black Warrior Review*. She holds an MFA in Creative Writing from CalArts and currently lives in Los Angeles where she is a co-curator for the feminist reading series Mommy, Mommy!, co-editor of the online journal *[out of nothing]*, and co-founder of the interdisciplinary arts organization Strophe.

Out Now:
Women Writing the Weird
Edited by Deb Hoag

WEIRD

1. *Eldritch:* suggesting the operation of supernatural influences; "an eldritch screech"; "the three weird sisters"; "stumps . . . had uncanny shapes as of monstrous creatures" --John Galsworthy; "an unearthly light"; "he could hear the unearthly scream of some curlew piercing the din" —Henry Kingsley

2. *Wyrd:* fate personified; any one of the three Weird Sisters

3. Strikingly odd or unusual; "some trick of the moonlight; some weird effect of shadow" —Bram Stoker

WEIRD FICTION

1. Stories that delight, surprise, that hang about the dusky edges of 'mainstream' fiction with characters, settings, plots that abandon the normal and mundane and explore new ideas, themes and ways of being. —Deb Hoag

RRP: £14.99 ($28.95).
Available: October 2011 (pre-orders from September 2011).

featuring
Nancy A. Collins, Eugie Foster, Janice Lee, Rachel Kendall, Candy Caradoc, Mysty Unger, Roberta Lawson, Sara Genge, Gina Ranalli, Deb Hoag, C. M. Vernon, Aliette de Bodard, Caroline M. Yoachim, Flavia Testa, Aimee C. Amodio, Ann Hagman Cardinal, Rachel Turner, Wendy Jane Muzlanova, Katie Coyle, Helen Burke, Janis Butler Holm, J.S. Breukelaar, Carol Novack, Tantra Bensko, Nancy DiMauro, and Moira McPartlin.

ND - #0445 - 270225 - C4 - 229/152/12 - PB - 9781907133053 - Matt Lamination